For Frances Collinson
and the children of
St Mary's Infant School,
Tetbury, Gloucestershire.
J.T.

To Oliver
S.G.

Also by Judy Taylor and Susan Gantner
Sophie and Jack
Sophie and Jack Help Out
Sophie and Jack in the Snow

British Library Cataloguing in Publication Data Taylor, Judy   Sophie and Jack in the rain.
I. Title II. Gantner, Susan   823'.914 [J] ISBN 0-370-31245-7

Printed in Great Britain by Cambus Litho, East Kilbride for The Bodley Head Ltd, 32 Bedford Square, London WC1B 3SG

First published 1989

JUDY TAYLOR

Sophie and Jack in the Rain

Illustrated by Susan Gantner

The Bodley Head
London

"I'm bored," said Jack.

"There's nothing to do," agreed Sophie.

"What about your new game?" asked Mama.

"I hope it's a quiet one," mumbled Papa.

Outside, a big tree had blown down in the storm.

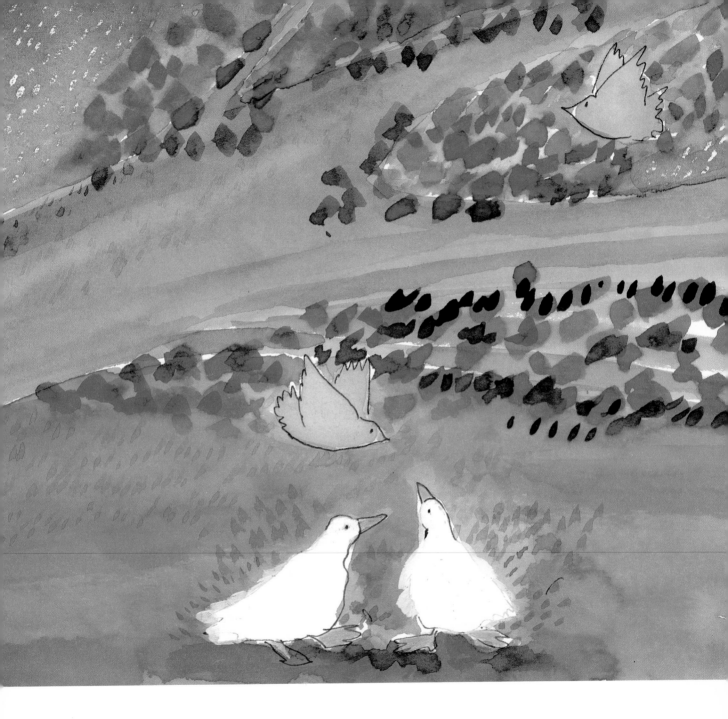

It was still raining hard.

"Let's go out," said Jack.

"Yes, in the rain!" said Sophie.

Jack jumped in the puddles.

Sophie splashed in the puddles.

"Let's climb," said Jack.

"Let's swing," said Sophie.

The rain kept falling.

It felt cool, cool.

"I'm an acrobat," boasted Jack.

"I'm an explorer," whispered Sophie.

"Time to come in," called Mama.

"And leave your boots outside, please."

"Here comes the sun!" said Jack.

"It makes everything sparkle," said Sophie.

High above the fallen tree

appeared a beautiful rainbow.

"Hip-hippo-ray!"

cheered Sophie and Jack together.